To the J Division: Jon, Jenny, Jack and James

Special thanks to Benjamin Scott

Bloomsbury Publishing, London, Berlin, New York and Sydney

First published in Great Britain in April 2012 by Bloomsbury Publishing Plc
50 Bedford Square, London, WC1B 3DP

Copyright © Working Partners Limited 2012
Illustrations copyright © Sam Hadley 2012

The moral rights of the author and illustrator have been asserted

A CIP catalogue record for this book is available from the British Library

ISBN 978 1 4088 1581 6

MIX
Paper from
responsible sources
FSC® C018072

Typeset by Hewer Text UK Ltd, Edinburgh
Printed in Great Britain by Clays Ltd, St Ives Plc, Bungay, Suffolk

1 3 5 7 9 10 8 6 4 2

www.bloomsbury.com
www.starfighterbooks.com

MAX CHASE

BLOOMSBURY

LONDON BERLIN NEW YORK SYDNEY

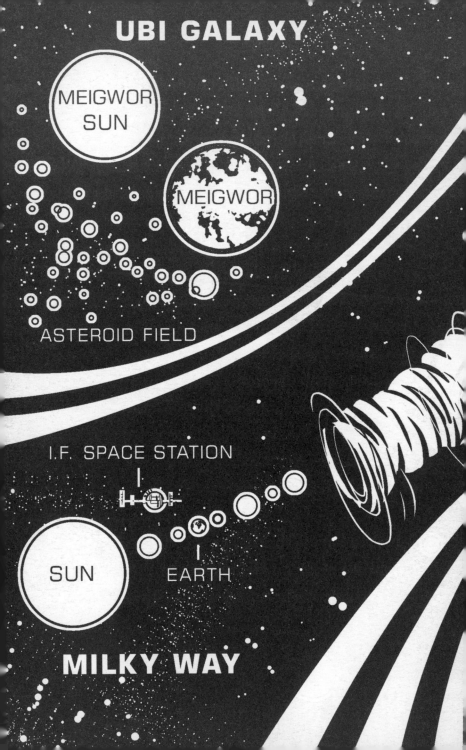

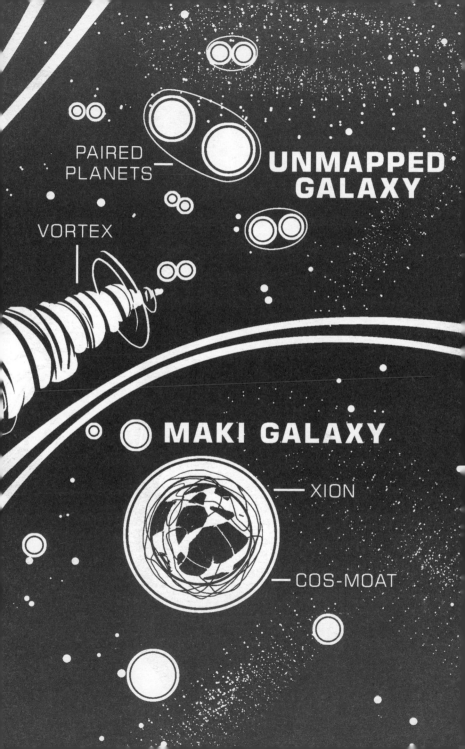

STAR FIGHTERS

An elite *fighting team* sworn to protect and defend the galaxy

It is the year 5012 and the Milky Way galaxy is under attack . . .

After the Universal War . . . a war that almost brought about the destruction of every known universe . . . the planets in the Milky Way banded together to create the Intergalactic Force – an elite fighting team sworn to protect and defend the galaxy.

Only the brightest and most promising students are accepted into the Intergalactic Force Academy, and only the very best cadets reach the highest of their ranks and become . . .

To be a Star Fighter is to dedicate your life to one mission: *Peace in Space*. They are given the coolest weapons, the fastest spaceships – and the most dangerous missions. Everyone at the Intergalactic Force Academy wants to be a Star Fighter someday.

Do YOU have what it takes?

Chapter 1

'We made it!' Diesel cheered. The gunner's narrow band of hair was a happy shade of orange. He wiggled around the Bridge in some strange Martian victory dance.

Even Otto, the Meigwor bounty hunter, looked on the verge of a little smile. His lipless mouth curled upwards like a dying space-slug.

Diesel whooped. 'If I wasn't the most amazing gunner in this galaxy, we'd never have got out of that alive.'

Otto's faint smile faltered. '*I* saved us!'

boomed the Meigwor. 'It was *my* skill that obliterated that massive rock!'

Diesel stopped dancing. His eyes flashed yellow. 'That wasn't skill, it was luck. If it wasn't for me, we'd have been smashed into oblivion.'

Peri couldn't help laughing. With those two arguing, everything was back to normal. Peri high-fived Selene, it was good to have their engineer back and safe. They'd rescued her from the Meigwors, refused to hand over Prince Onix and made a lucky escape from Otto's home planet. The vengeful Meigwor General Rouwgim had created a giant asteroid storm and it had been a team effort to guide the *Phoenix* through it without being pulverised. Diesel and Otto had blasted what they could, while Peri and Selene had navigated the *Phoenix* through the deadly shower of rocks.

'I'll check the damage, while you plan our next move,' Selene said.

Peri smiled. Selene's time in captivity had done nothing for her bossiness. She was even back in her patched spacesuit and had a smudge of grease on her cheek.

'Otto, Diesel, stop arguing,' she snapped. 'I need you to check over the weapons systems to see what needs to be repaired first.' The two gunners glared at her but knew better than to argue. They slouched to the gunnery station.

'Onix,' Selene continued as she pushed past the prince, 'try to stay out of the way.'

'No one talks to the firstborn son and heir to the throne of Xion like that!' the prince said, stiffening, and slicked his webbed fingers through his hair. 'Especially not a girl.'

Peri winced. Onix was in really big trouble. He didn't know Selene. She could use most of the weapons on the *Phoenix,* and she didn't like being treated like a girl. Selene's eyes narrowed like the focusing lens on a DeathRay pulveriser. 'I'm the engineer of this ship and you'll do what you're told or you can find another ride home.'

Onix didn't say a word, but moved as far away from her as he could.

'Right,' Peri said. 'Our priority is to return Prince Onix to Xion.'

'No! We must return to Earth!' Diesel yelled. 'The emperor will be missing me . . . I mean, us! Earth needs its best Star Fighters back.'

Selene adjusted some nano-dials on the control panel. 'Maybe the prince can tell Xion to stop attacking the Milky Way. Then we can go home.'

Peri clicked his fingers and the control panel slipped from under Selene's hands. It floated towards him. 'First,' he said, 'let's contact Xion and explain that kidnapping Onix was a mistake. We don't need a second planet after us.'

Peri activated the com-pad, flicking a zip-dial to scan all frequencies and automatically connect with planet Xion.

'Hold it!' Otto boomed. 'The Xions will take me prisoner!'

'I'll make sure you get far worse,' mumbled Onix, 'you muscle-bound Meigwor freak.'

Otto pulled a short silver stick from his snakeskin belt and stepped towards the prince. 'What was that, squid-breath? You think these pathetic Earthlings are going to defend *you*?'

'Pathetic?!' Diesel shouted. 'We could beat the entire Meigwor space fleet without breaking a sweat.'

Otto's black tongue shot out and cracked

like a whip in front of Diesel's nose. 'Stay out of it, space-monkey!'

'Never!' Diesel launched himself, grabbing the two lumps on Otto's freakishly long neck as Onix leapt on to the Meigwor's legs. Otto staggered backwards until he lost his balance. Peri sprang from the captain's chair to avoid being hit, but one of Otto's double-jointed elbows slammed into Peri's chest and pinned him against the deck.

'Cosmic squid-brains!' Otto roared. 'Space-monkey slime!'

Peri scrambled free from the fight. Diesel was darting and weaving and trying to punch Otto wherever he could. Otto was trying to shake Onix from his back, but the prince clung on like a space-limpet.

'Meigwor scum,' the prince yelled, as gobs of fishy sweat flew off him. 'Lumpy-necked space-freak!'

Otto was flailing around trying to hit both of them with the silver stick. The weapon was now eleven times longer than it had been. As the Meigwor waved it about, sparks flew everywhere.

Whaacckk! The stick smacked against Peri's arm.

Craackle. A zap of electricity fizzed through him. His muscles and computer circuits twitched uncontrollably, making his eyes water as his vision shimmered. *The stick is an electro-prod!* he realised.

'Stop it now, before someone gets hurt,' Peri yelled, dodging Otto's electro-prod, Diesel's fists and Onix's sweat. Otto threw Onix from his back, before knocking Diesel and Peri to the deck and pouncing on them. It was going to be hard to break up the fight alone.

'Selene – help!' Peri called.

Peri saw the engineer grab what looked like a ten-centimetre-square piece of pink paper from her tool belt. She dashed towards the prince as he stood up, ready to rejoin the fight. She slapped the paper on his forehead and it stuck. Onix stumbled backwards looking stunned.

'One down, two to go,' Selene muttered, as the prince fell face first on to the deck. 'Sleep well, Your *Highness*.'

'Who's next?' Selene asked and looked from Diesel to Otto. The pair stopped struggling as they glanced at Onix's limp body.

Peri wrestled free from under them and rushed over to the prince. Onix was out cold. 'What have you done?'

Selene snatched the sticky paper from the prince's forehead. 'I call it a Sleepez. Something I invented myself,' she said proudly. 'The adhesive is a sedative. The prince will be out for a few hours.'

'Hours?' Peri said, shaking the prince.

'He got what he deserved,' Selene replied.

'His Royal Majesty, King of Xion,' announced the ship.

Peri looked up. The face of the Xion king dominated the 360-monitor. For a nanosecond, the king looked curious – but then his expression changed to shock and horror. Peri's circuits chilled as he realised what the scene on the Bridge must look like to the king. Peri was kneeling over an unconscious Onix, shaking him.

'What have you done to my son?' the king shouted.

'No,' said Peri, standing up. 'Wait! You don't understand.'

The king looked so angry; Peri felt as if his voice might rattle the *Phoenix*, even from light years away. 'Wicked aliens! You taunt me with my son's dead body! Xion won't stand it! You will pay for this . . . *with your lives!*'

'He's not dead!' Diesel shouted. 'Selene just knocked him out!'

'Shut up, Diesel, and wake him up,' Peri hissed as he tried to block the king's view of Onix. 'Get Otto to help.'

'Your Majesty,' Peri addressed the king. 'We've just prevented your son from falling into the hands of the Meigwors.'

'Lies!' screamed the king. 'I can see a Meigwor behind you, torturing my son!'

Peri spun around. Diesel and Otto had each grabbed hold of either end of the prince and were trying to tug him from the other's grasp.

'You're going to kill him!' Otto boomed, pulling on the prince's legs.

'Give him to me,' yelled Diesel, yanking Onix back. 'I got top marks in my medical treatment exam.'

'Never!' Otto yelled. 'I'll cure the Xions, once and for all!'

'Stop it!' Peri shouted at them. 'This isn't a tug of war.' He spun round again, realising the king was watching everything. 'Wait, they're not torturing him.'

But the king had made up his mind. 'My son's death will be avenged,' he shouted. 'Let's see if your fancy ship can escape the

entire Xion fleet!' His eyes turned to someone off-screen. 'Launch all the Deathray transporters, ready the battleships, orders to destroy!'

'No,' said Peri, 'you must listen to —'

But the king had vanished. Peri activated the Velocity View. The long curved monitor whirled from the back of the control panel. It pulsed to life and showed a mass of green dots swarming from Onix's home planet. Peri could imagine every ship in the fleet heading straight for the *Phoenix*.

Selene pulled a small pen-like object from her tool belt and fired a bright yellow laser beam at the prince.

'Don't make it worse!' Peri shouted.

'I'm not,' she replied, as she finished tracing a line around the prince's body. The yellow light melted over Onix and he disappeared. 'I've sent the prince to the Med Centre, out of harm's way.'

Diesel tugged at the sleeve of Peri's Expedition Wear.

'What is it?' Peri asked.

Diesel pointed to the Velocity View. A cluster of red dots were also approaching the *Phoenix*. 'The Meigwors have found us too!'

Chapter 2

Blip. Blip-Blip. Blip-Blip-Blip. Green lights flashed over the Velocity View as more Xion ships appeared.

Ping. Ping-Ping. Ping-Ping-Ping. Red lights swarmed across the screen from the other side of the universe as Meigwor ships appeared.

Peri shook his head. Hundreds of battle-ships, fighters and destroyers filled the screen.

And they were all gunning for the *Phoenix*.

Peri couldn't remember worse odds in a

battle scenario — not in any of the galactic-war class simulations he'd sat through or the *Explosive Book of Space Battles.*

Otto and Diesel leapt to the gunnery station. Diesel smacked a switch and the floating console expanded to reveal further rows of triggers, 3-D target trackers and X-plode detonators. Diesel cracked his knuckles as he looked over the weapons systems.

Peri and Selene slipped into the two captain's chairs. Astro-harnesses snaked round them. Peri gripped the Nav-wheel.

'Get ready,' shouted Selene. 'Incoming!'

Twenty-two Meigwor fighter pods were on a fast-approach. They were like giant cobra-heads, flying in a perfect V-formation. But instead of fangs, the cobra-heads had ultra-accurate lasers. Peri jerked the Nav-wheel and pulled the thrusters hard, trying to get beyond their weapons' range.

He wasn't fast enough. The Meigwors opened fire. Brilliant orange lasers criss-crossed the black space. Their complicated firing pattern left little room for manoeuvring – even for the most brilliant ship in the Milky Way. Peri banked hard, pushing the thrusters to maximum.

But no sooner had they dodged the first round of laser fire, when Selene shouted, 'Xion ships within firing range!'

The Xions' massive spherical battleships had their weapons ready. Pulverising Death-Rays and cluster missiles burst from huge spikes in their hulls. Peri slammed on the dodge mechanism to avoid being hit. The ship shifted to the right as the missiles burst past. He twisted the Nav-wheel to escape the other weapons, but too many vessels were firing.

Ziiing-frroooaaarr! A DeathRay glanced off the port shield, spinning the *Phoenix* with the force of its blast. Peri yanked the anti-drift levers, fighting to gain control. As the ship stopped spinning, he kicked the thrusters hard. The *Phoenix* shot forward, but a missile slammed into it and exploded against the shields. *Shhhaaablllaaammm!*

Peri was thrown against his astro-harness. Warning lights flashed across the entire control panel. The shield's protective power was dropping to dangerous levels.

He didn't know how many more hits the ship could take.

'Weapons lock on Xion target!' Otto cheered from his gunner's station. 'Watch me blast their ship into another universe.'

'Hold fire,' Peri ordered, smacking the turbo-reverse to stop another cluster missile from slamming into the *Phoenix*. 'Don't shoot the Xions. It's just a misunderstanding!'

Kaaaaboooom! The ship shook again as the missile exploded close by.

'Are you mad, space-monkey?!' Otto boomed. 'We *must* fire back. And I have got a clear shot!'

'No, Peri is right,' Selene said. 'They'll never believe our story if we shoot back. It'll make things worse.'

Otto slapped the side of the gunnery station angrily. 'Worse? They're already shooting at us!'

'Peri,' Diesel shouted. 'I've got a clear shot. Permission to vaporise the Meigwor fighter!'

'Permission granted,' Peri replied.

'What?! NO!' Otto's lumps twitched. 'What happened to not making a bad situation worse?'

Peri stared at the blobs on the Velocity View screen. He didn't want to admit it, but Otto was right. Blasting ships from space just because he didn't like those particular aliens was wrong. They shouldn't be destroying anything, unless they had no choice. *Star Fighters save planets, they don't destroy them*, he thought.

'Otto's right,' Peri said. 'Hold your fire. We should evade — let's go Superluminal!'

'We can't!' Selene exclaimed. 'The *Phoenix* is still rejuvenating from escaping the asteroid belt. It needs all its power to keep the shields up.' She pushed her hair back and stared at the console. 'Just give me a minute.'

'We don't have time,' Diesel shouted. 'We're going to be obliterated any moment.'

'I know!' she screamed. 'Let me think.'

Selene hit the console. 'That's it! I've just got to re-route power to the ship's cloak,' she said, almost as fast as her hands blurring over the controls. 'And make an adjustment so we don't show up on any space-wake scanners. There!'

Suddenly, the Xions and the Meigwors stopped firing.

'We did it!' Selene punched the air.

'Great,' said Peri. 'Except . . . If we're no longer between the Meigwors and the Xions, then the only thing they can see is each other.'

Diesel gulped. 'They'll open fire –'

Selene put her head in her hands. 'And we'll be caught in the middle.'

'We've got to get out of here now!' Peri yelled.

But it was already too late. The two enemy fleets launched every weapon in their extensive arsenals. Ships exploded on both sides.

The *Phoenix* was an invisible sitting duck.

With thrusters at maximum, Peri dodged missiles, DeathRays and fighter drones. The alien ships had broken formation, attacking each other in ship-to-ship combat. As long as they remained distracted, he hoped he could creep the *Phoenix* safely through the warzone.

Peri swung the vessel out of the path of a Meigwor viper-ship, pursued by a dozen Xion fighter craft. Otto gripped the sides of the gunnery station. The patches around his eyes grew darker and darker.

Suddenly, a pulverising DeathRay lit up the monitor and the Meigwor ship exploded into a gazillion pieces.

'Stinking Xion,' Otto yelled, as his hands darted across the gunnery station. Peri saw the *Phoenix* spit a hail of missiles at the Xion ships.

'Otto, no!' he shouted, but warnings were already flashing across the control panel. 'If we fire, then the other ships can pinpoint our –'

Kllaaablaam! The *Phoenix* shook as a DeathRay made a direct hit.

'We've lost the cloak,' Selene screamed.

'Multiple weapons lock,' the *Phoenix* reported. 'Evasive manoeuvres advised. Nice day to go surfing.'

Peri wondered if that last blast had

scrambled the ship's logic-circuits. But as he jammed on the hyper-brakes and spun the ship around, he understood what the *Phoenix* was suggesting . . .

The alien ships opened fire on their position. Peri kicked the thrusters beyond maximum and moments later, DeathRays, cluster missiles and BlastBeams exploded barely a fraction behind them. It was like a sun going supernova!

A massive shockwave smacked into them, catapulting them away from the fiery explosion. Peri tried to surf the wave as the *Phoenix* had suggested, but it was too powerful. The ship was spinning out of control. Even the UpRighter mechanism strained against the forces battering the ship, letting the Bridge tip one way, then another. Peri clung on to the Nav-wheel, glad for his astro-harness.

'Gravitational pull detected,' the *Phoenix* announced.

'That can't be right,' Diesel shouted. 'There's nothing here.'

'Just because you can't see it, doesn't mean there's nothing there,' Selene answered. 'We're being sucked into a planet.'

Peri felt a tingle of electric dread. 'And we can't do anything to stop it!'

Chapter 3

Eeeeee-rraaaaraa!

As alarms blared across the Bridge, robotic arms shot down from the ceiling. A pair of pinch-grips yanked Peri away from the controls. 'Preparing for crash landing,' the ship announced.

'Get off,' Peri shouted as the *Phoenix* hoisted him into the air. He tried to wriggle free, but the ship held him and the others tightly. Otto and Selene were slipped into Expedition Wear. Sleek survival podpacks were strapped to everyone's shoulders.

Light steel cable snaked down from the ceiling and darted towards the podpacks. They attached themselves with a *sssurpt!* Transparent helmets sprang from the suit collars, sealing them in. A huge portal as large as a spaceball goalmouth opened above them. The sound of roaring air filled the Bridge.

The cable attached to his podpack was twitching. Peri had a bad feeling about this.

'Ohhh nooo!' he screamed, as a hatch opened and the cable threw him and the rest of his crew out of the *Phoenix*. The ship must have calculated that their chances of survival would be greater if it ejected them before impact.

Peri's Expedition Wear hissed and whirred, tightening as it inflated to form a bubble of translucent material. He could now see that the *Phoenix* was speeding

towards a small moon-planet. The combined radiation of its twin suns must have made it dark to the ship's sensors. Peri was floating down towards its flat sandy surface. He looked for signs of civilisation, but saw none – the moon-planet seemed uninhabited.

Neeaaawww-Kaaaccchhhaaam!

Peri watched with horror as the *Phoenix* punched a crater in the surface before gouging a trench into the sand. He hoped the landing hadn't damaged the ship beyond repair, but it was the least of his worries. He had picked up speed and was falling fast. He looked to his crew for help, but they too were plummeting towards the ground.

Peri closed his eyes, bracing himself for the impact.

Boin-n-n-g!

He risked opening his eyes. 'Cosmo-cool!'

He laughed. In his inflated Expedition Wear, he had bounced like a spaceball, spinning as he moved over the moon-planet's white sand. He could see the others bouncing close by.

'Isn't this great, Peri?' Selene crackled across the radio. 'The suits are . . . *crrrrk* . . . designed to withstand the impact. The surface tension creates —'

'Awful way to travel!' boomed Otto, his bubble bashing into Peri's. 'The sooner —'

A loud groan cut him short. 'I think I'm going to puke,' Diesel said over the radio.

'Not in your helmet,' Selene retorted. 'You don't want . . . *crrrrk* . . . over your face.'

Peri's survival bubble deflated so he could land on the planet's powdery surface. *Hissssss.* The Expedition Wear returned to its normal shape. Instantly, the suit turned red which meant the planet was colder than the interior of the *Phoenix*. His boots widened to stop him sinking into the sand.

Diesel was doubled over with motion sickness. His narrow band of hair had turned green and was lying flat on his head. 'Let's just get back to the ship,' he moaned, pinching his lips together tightly.

Peri spotted Otto. Even though the Expedition Wear had expanded to accommodate Otto's strange shape, his spacesuit looked as if it was bursting at the seams. His neck was squashed in his helmet and his arms folded awkwardly in his sleeves. Otto shivered. 'The space-monkey's right . . . Too c-c-cold!'

For once Peri agreed with the gunners. 'We'd better find the *Phoenix* and see what the damage is,' Peri replied. 'Luckily, we're still connected to the ship like space-pets on a lead.'

Peri followed the cable connected to his podpack over the shifting sands. He saw a plume of black smoke rising over the next sand dune and broke into a run. As he scrambled down the dune, he could see the shell of their once sleek white vessel was blackened and dented. It creaked and made strange electrical crackling sounds.

Peri put his hand on the ship's charred surface and waited for the ghostly green light to trace his palm. Nothing. 'This is bad,' he muttered.

'Let me try,' said Selene, but as soon as she touched the ship she leapt back. 'Ouch. It just stung me. The *Phoenix* doesn't want us to go inside.'

'It doesn't want *you* to go inside,' said Diesel. 'I'm the most important person on the crew. It won't refuse me.'

Diesel took a step towards the ship,

walking straight into a bolt of electricity from the spaceship's hull. His hair fanned out from the static.

'Serves you right,' Peri chuckled.

'Self-repair activated,' the *Phoenix* reported calmly. 'Energy levels critical. All power diverted to essential subroutines.'

'Until the damage is repaired, we're stuck out here,' Selene explained. 'Using life support would just drain the *Phoenix*'s energy reserves.'

'But what about Prince Onix?' Peri asked. 'He's still on board.'

'Alien specimen from Xion placed in rejuvenating coma,' the ship answered. 'He will remain unconscious until fully recovered.'

'Thank you, *Phoenix*.' Peri looked over the sandy dunes surrounding them. 'Well . . . let's find some shelter.'

'No, let's *explore*,' said Selene.

'Explore *what?*' Diesel asked. 'Moon-planets are never inhabited. I vote we stay put.'

'I ag-ag-agreeee!' Otto stuttered. His freakishly long neck had shrunk to half its size. The Meigwor was not suited for the cold. 'Expedition Wear not w-w-warm enough.'

'Stay here, then,' Selene said, 'But the *Phoenix* won't be repaired for a while, and how often do you get to explore a moon-planet?'

Peri and Selene walked along the trench created by the *Phoenix*. They were still tethered to the ship, so they wouldn't be able to go far. Diesel and Otto were behind them. The Meigwor's normally brisk walk had been reduced to a shuffle.

Peri was amazed at the vast emptiness of the moon-planet. The two suns were setting, casting a strange red glow over the horizon.

'Look at that crater,' Selene exclaimed.

Peri stared where Selene pointed. It was as though a giant moon-eating grub had bitten into the planet. Debris was piled all around it. 'This is our fault,' Peri muttered. 'When the *Phoenix* crashed into the planet, it punched a crater into the –'

'We didn't make this,' Selene interrupted. 'Look around you. Someone's been drilling for fuel here.'

Peri looked up and saw a sea of craters stretching out towards the horizon, dotted with hunks of rusting machinery. He ran to the nearest crater to have a closer look. Strange, jagged black stones stuck out of the crater's edge. An electric charge of anger surged through Peri. 'Drilling for fuel! Why can't species just leave places like this alone?'

Peri stared into the hole. It was still crumbling inwards and getting bigger.

A strange rumbling came from deep within the crater, followed by an eerie cry.

'Can you hear that?' Peri asked.

'It's probably the ground shifting,' said Diesel, pushing Peri aside to look. 'The gravitational pull of the twin suns must have destabilised its core. Basic astrogeology, for which I have a natural talent.'

Otto finally lumbered up next to them,

muttering, 'H-H-Hate . . . c-c-cold!' He bent over, stretching out his hands. 'Black rock! Very valuable.' He tucked a handful of shiny black stones into the pocket of his Expedition Wear, before extending his arms as far as they would reach for more. But the rock was still another hand's length away. As Otto edged forward, the sandy edge of the crater collapsed.

'*Scrofa-ahhhggg!*' he screamed as he tumbled into the hole.

'Well that solves one problem nicely,' Diesel said, smirking, before the ground gave way beneath him. '*Mh'nak!*'

'Diesel!' Peri shouted, holding out his hand and leaning over the edge. He felt Diesel's fingers slip through his own, before he too was falling down the stony sides of the crater.

Chapter 4

Peri clawed against the tumbling rocks and sand, but nothing could stop him.

Ooomph! Peri hit a hard black surface and continued falling. He had landed at the top of a chute in the wall of the crater made from the black stone. He turned on to his back and picked up speed, sliding feet-first. He zoomed faster and faster until he was *swoosh-ing* down the tunnel, in which he was thrown left, then right, then spun 360 degrees.

'Whooo-hooo!' Peri cheered. Then, a second later: 'Oh no!'

Suddenly, Peri was dropping faster than a lead spaceship in a gravity-hole. He screamed as his circuits crackled with fear. His stomach felt as though it had been left behind as he plummeted through the pitch-black.

Hummppff! Peri jerked to a halt as the cable connecting him to the *Phoenix* tugged him back. It had reached its maximum length, but before he could get his breath back, he heard the cable snap.

Peri tensed his muscles and prepared to smack into the ground, then he heard a whirr and hum. His Expedition Wear sprang into action, inflating into a giant bubble again.

He still couldn't see where he was falling. It was too dark to know if the Expedition Wear could save him, or if he would end up impaled on a stony spike. But as he hit the ground, the inflated suit flung him up into the air again, unharmed. He kept bouncing, unable to do anything until the momentum from the fall ran out and his suit deflated.

It was totally dark. He ran his fingers over the suit's control panel, but didn't know which button to press. Before he could figure out which one would help him see in the dark, he heard something landing nearby, followed by the hiss of more Expedition Wear deflating.

Otto's voice was the first he heard. 'I told you w-w-we should have stayed with the sh-sh-ship!'

Diesel gasped. 'Something just brushed against me! Monster alert!'

'That was *me*, you dumboid,' Selene said.

'How do I activate my suit to see in the dark?' Peri asked.

'I think they got damaged in the fall,' Diesel cried. 'Wait, something's happening to mine, it's lighting up like a Zero-G firework display.'

Whatever was happening to Diesel's suit was happening to Peri's too. His helmet hummed as dark green clouds of pixels flickered over his visor. As they danced across Peri's vision, the electronic cloud grew steadily brighter like watching a star explode in ultra-ultra-slow motion. Shapes began appearing in the darkness until he could see Selene, Diesel and Otto standing next to him. Except – they were green.

'Night-vision-coated visors!' Selene cheered. 'Expedition Wear can do everything.'

Peri was pleased the Expedition Wear had saved him again, but they were still stranded at the bottom of a gigantic cavern. The walls were made from the same black shiny stone Otto had spotted at the surface of the planet, but this rock was worn smooth. Paths led in every direction, disappearing into black openings in the cavern wall.

'We must be in a vast network of underground tunnels,' Peri said as he peered around. He looked up and saw the four steel cables dangling over the edge of the hole, but the severed cables were too high to reach.

'Any ideas how we can reach them?' he asked.

'Let's bl-bl-blast our way back to the s-s-surface!' Otto boomed, trying not to shiver.

'And cause another cave-in?' Peri shook his head. 'While I'm in charge, we're going to find a less dangerous way.'

'Who put you in ch-ch-charge?!' Otto demanded.

'Yeah,' Diesel said, pressing a button on his Expedition Wear. A stick of Eterni-chew gum sprang from the edge of the helmet into his mouth. 'I should be . . . *schliip* . . . in charge. I scored the . . . *schliip* . . . best on my leadership . . . *schliip* . . . exams at the Academy.'

'Don't talk and chew,' Selene snapped. 'It doesn't matter who's in charge. We still need a –'

A deep noise echoed around the cavern. It was a cross between a rumble and a low-pitched squeak. It made Peri's circuits tingle with fear. 'I don't like the sound of that.'

'We should check it out,' Selene said. 'You never know what we could discover. Maybe a brand-new species, unknown to science.'

'That's probably because the scientists get eaten before they find out,' Diesel muttered.

'No one in their right mind g-g-goes towards scary noises inside dark c-c-caves!' Otto said irritably. 'It's the w-w-worst suggestion I've ever heard! No wonder your sp-sp-species is so inferior – you have no survival i-i-instincts!'

'Don't speak for me . . . *schliip* . . . lamiz-oid,' said Diesel as he chewed. 'I've got enough survival instincts to fill a galaxy.'

'We should concentrate on getting out of here, not discovering new species,' said Peri.

'What if the creature making that noise can help us?' Selene asked. 'We don't have any better ideas right now.'

She had a point. 'OK,' Peri said. 'Set your SpeakEasy to scan. If the creatures can talk, the SpeakEasy will translate for us.'

Peri pressed his fingers against the bottom of his helmet. The Expedition Wear softened and moulded around his hands, allowing him to press the bulge under his chin. A roar of static filled his head as the SpeakEasy was activated. The standard-issue implant for IF cadets allowed him and Diesel to talk and understand every language in the universe. Selene had a makeshift SpeakEasy device strapped to her chin that she had rigged herself. She might not have been a real IF cadet, but Peri thought she deserved to be.

He listened as the static faded, but nothing else seemed to come through the device.

'Sorry, Selene,' said Peri. 'I don't think –'

'Heat.'

Peri winced at the chorus of voices echoing around his helmet. He looked at Diesel, trying to see if he had heard it too. The half-Martian had his mouth open in surprise, a wad of Eterni-chew hanging from a tooth. Selene looked shocked as well. Otto either hadn't heard or didn't care.

'What was that?' Peri asked.

'Heat,' the voices chorused again, this time accompanied by the crackle of the radio.

'It's coming through the SpeakEasy device,' Diesel exclaimed.

'It seems to be coming from down there.' Selene pointed behind her.

Peri peered down the tunnel for the source of the voices. A strange flickering white-green cloud appeared from the darkness. But when it got closer, Peri realised this was not a single, writhing shape. It was many, many creatures – heading right for them.

Selene gasped. 'Moon-bats!'

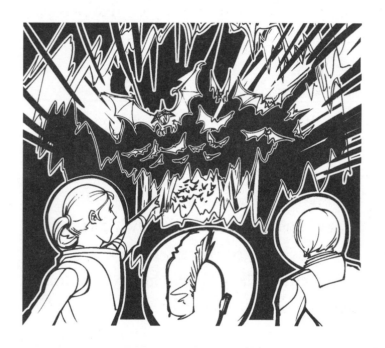

Chapter 5

The swarm of moon-bats swooped out of the tunnel with ear-splitting screeches. Thousands of them filled the cavern, swirling and turning in tight circles to stay aloft. They created gusts of wind which buffeted Peri's Expedition Wear. Their wings were lined with spikes. Their hairless, wrinkled faces opened to reveal fangs the size of Peri's fingers.

Peri ducked as a bat sliced past too close for comfort. 'Let's get out of here!'

'This way!' Otto yelled, heading down the

nearest tunnel, leading Diesel and Selene.

Peri set off after them, knowing their suits would tear and they would suffocate if the moon-bats got too close with their sharp spikes and razor-like fangs.

His SpeakEasy crackled. 'Heat!' It screamed straight into his brain.

The closer the bats came, the louder the voices got.

He could see Selene ahead of him. The wind nudging him from behind was getting stronger. The bats had nearly reached them. They were going to crash straight into him and his crew.

Peri dived forward. He grabbed Selene, tackling her to the floor. Like dominoes, Selene toppled Diesel, who floored Otto in turn. As the *Phoenix*'s crew crashed into the ground, the swarm of moon-bats passed overhead.

'That was close,' Peri said, helping Selene and Diesel to stand.

But he spoke too soon. The bats had swerved around like cosmic-boomerangs and were spinning fiercely back towards them.

'Retreat!' Peri shouted and sprinted as fast as he could back the way they had come. A narrow shaft of sunlight was now streaming into the cave through the hole in the ceiling. It sliced the cave in two, one side lit and the other dark. Rock and sand were still crumbling down as the hole above them got bigger.

'The planet must have rotated to the perfect angle for one of the suns to shine in,' Selene said.

'Against the w-w-wall!' Otto boomed. As he stepped into the light half of the cave, it made his helmet shine like a halo. He pulled his weapon from his belt. 'Let's bl-bl-blast the bats!'

'No, Otto!' Peri cried, pulling Selene and Diesel into the beam of light next to the bounty hunter. 'Don't shoot.'

Although the swirling mass got larger and larger, not a single bat crossed the beam of light. Their screeches grew louder.

The whole swarm hovered in the air as though suspended in zero gravity. Peri wondered what the bats were trying to do. What if they weren't attacking? Perhaps they were scared. They hadn't actually hurt him or his friends.

That's it! Peri realised. The bats were not crossing the beam of light. The light was as scary to them as the dark was to him. The creatures started repeating a new phrase: 'Frightened, frightened.'

Peri gestured for Selene, Diesel and Otto to come closer to him.

'I don't think the bats are trying to attack

us,' Peri told them. 'They're frightened and scared of the heat from the sunlight. I think they're asking for help . . .'

'I don't understand,' Diesel said. 'Why don't they just tell us what's wrong instead of repeating the same words over and over again?'

'I'm guessing that they don't have their own language,' Peri replied. 'The SpeakEasy must be picking up on their basic emotions.'

Selene nodded. 'In which case, the SpeakEasy should be able to help transmit our emotions to them.'

'We could try to talk to them,' Peri said.

Otto sneered. 'You can't talk with these blood s-s-suckers!'

'This is crazy.' Diesel jabbed the side of Peri's suit. 'What if the bats are tricking us? Perhaps they just want us to move away from the light so that they can have us for dinner. One of us should try to climb out and use the *Phoenix* to rescue the others before we become bat biscuits.'

'The space-monkey makes sense!' Otto boomed. 'I'm the most fr-fr-frozen, so I should go get the ship!'

'No!' chorused Peri, Diesel and Selene.

'You've got to be kidding,' Peri continued. 'You'd steal the ship and take Prince Onix without a second thought for us.'

Diesel nodded inside his helmet. 'You'd leave us to the moon-bats.'

Selene crossed her arms. 'Definitely.'

'The thought n-n-never crossed my mind!' Otto said, but the grin on his lipless mouth said otherwise.

'We can't just leave. We're IF cadets,' Peri said. 'These creatures need our help. I'm going to find out what I can, and see if I can fix the problem. Who's with me?'

Diesel shook his head. 'You've got that look on your face. Typical first year. Just because someone else has a problem doesn't mean you have to solve it. Leave it for someone else to fix.'

'Diesel,' Peri said calmly. 'We fled our home because the Milky Way was under attack. You know what it's like to be scared. We've got to at least try to do something to help.'

'I hate it when you're right,' Diesel grumbled. 'You know I got top marks in my intergalactic ethics exam. You're not the only one who can care about this stupid stuff.'

'Now we're agreed,' Peri said, 'how do we communicate with the moon-bats?'

'Like I said, they won't understand your words but they might feel your emotion,' Selene said. 'Talk simply and directly.'

Peri took a deep breath. He had to tell the bats his crew meant no harm and that they were going to help. *No,* he thought, *it's got to be simple and direct.* He stepped through the beam of light towards the bats. They squeaked and swooped around his head.

'Tell us what is wrong,' Peri said slowly and clearly.

The bats kept slicing closer and closer. 'Heat! Frightened!' they cried.

'You've got to *feel* it,' Selene called. 'Project the feeling behind the words, don't just shout. They won't understand the words, only the emotion.'

Peri took another breath and calmed himself. Ignoring the bats' agitation, he forced himself to speak softly, imagining the calmness the bats must feel in complete darkness. He imagined himself going to sleep back on Earth, when his parents would wish him cosmic dreams. 'Peace,' he whispered. 'Peace.'

The bats softened their movements and began to hover around him. The aggression left their eyes.

'Friend,' Peri said.

'Melting,' the bats replied. 'Flood.'

Chapter 6

The moon-bats swirled around Peri, but didn't come closer.

'Melting,' the bats chorused. 'Flood.'

I don't understand, Peri thought, staring up at the green cloud of bats. The spikes on their fixed wings had stopped bristling, but they still looked sharp enough to hurt. 'What do you mean?'

It's no good, Peri thought, *the bats don't under-stand my question. I have to try something different.*

'Show us,' Peri said, but he knew he needed to project emotion into his words. He had to express the feeling, what it felt like to share. He conjured up the memory of telling Diesel about his bionic abilities after they had accidentally kidnapped the prince. It had been a relief to share his secret. He concentrated on the feeling and said, 'Show us.'

As one, the swarm turned. Their movements created a gust of wind that not only held them up but swept them towards a tunnel. They had understood!

'Q-q-quick, let's get out of h-h-here!' Otto stammered. 'B-b-before they return!'

'No,' Peri replied. 'I told the bats we would help them.'

'They're just b-b-bats!' Otto snorted. 'You soft-hearted air-breather!'

Peri had had enough of Otto's snide remarks. He didn't care if the Meigwor helped or not, he was going to find out what was frightening the moon-bats and help them, if he could. He started off down the tunnel where the creatures had flown.

His night-vision visor made the walls of the tunnel glint with green as if the rock was embedded with emeralds. But as Peri touched them he found the walls were slick with water. His space boots had already grown thick rubber soles to help him grip the wet floor.

'Come on,' Selene said, over the radio, 'Let's follow Peri before we lose him.'

'Peri's a . . . *crrrk* . . . if he thinks this is going to end well,' Diesel complained. 'You don't have to be as clever as me to know this is a bad idea.'

'Come on, Otto,' Selene radioed, 'or we'll leave you behind.'

Peri stumbled on. The bats were turning a corner. He could see the last few gliding out of sight. He tried running, but the tunnels were smooth as if worn down over the years. Even his boots struggled not to let him slip on the slippery surfaces.

'I say r-r-roast them with our lasers and e-e-eat them!' Otto grumbled, over the radio. 'They'd g-g-go well with s-s-sauce made from broccoli-caterpillars and sl-sl-slime-bugs!'

'Gross!' Peri, Selene and Diesel agreed.

The bats cries had faded, but the *Phoenix* crew could still make out two words clearly. 'Melting. Flood.'

Diesel's teeth were chattering. 'How can this planet be melting if it's made of sand and rock?'

'Just keep going,' Peri answered, over the radio.

But it is *odd*, Peri thought. It was getting colder and colder as they walked through the network of tunnels. His Expedition Wear glowed red in its struggle to keep him warm.

'Otto, keep up,' Selene ordered.

'Watch it, sp-sp-space-monkey!' Otto growled. 'Meigwors can't t-t-take the c-c-cold. I'm going as fast as I c-c-can!'

The tunnels looked super eerie through the night-vision visor. Strange formations along the wall glistened like Centori snot monsters. Peri touched one and felt water trickle over his gloves. The coldness from the ice underneath radiated through his Expedition Wear.

'Ice!' Peri exclaimed. 'No wonder the moon-planet's melting. It must have ice running through it.'

Peri pushed on. The rocky floor was getting wetter and wetter. The tunnel was getting steeper. He slipped and fell to his knees. The floor was cold and wet.

He reached for an icicle to pull himself up, but it snapped in his hand. He could see some sort of alien eyeball frozen into the ice. It stared back at him. Peri suppressed a scream and threw the icicle away. He wiped his hands against his suit. He didn't know what prey the bats ate, but he hoped it wasn't IF cadets! He had to trust the bats. He had no idea where they were taking him, but he didn't want to lose them in the maze of tunnels.

Peri caught up with the bats just as they swarmed into an enormous cavern. More bats were flying in from other tunnels, joining the masses already swirling above. There were perhaps a hundred, if not a thousand, times more bats than he had been following.

This must be where they roost, he thought.

He stood on the edge of a huge cavern of ice. It was almost perfectly cylindrical, like a missile-launch tube. He couldn't see how high it was because of the mass of circling bats. The walls were patterned with intricate crystalline shapes – from jagged stars, to long sharp lines that overlapped like laser fire. Each shape was coloured every imaginable shade of green in his night vision.

Peri stepped forward to see more clearly, but his foot found nothing but air! He threw his arms backwards, trying to shift his weight behind him. For a second, he tottered on the edge, his arms frantically waving, before tipping himself back on to the path.

He stared into the abyss below, his heart somersaulting. It had been a narrow escape.

The path didn't continue straight into the cave. It branched off in both directions around the edges of the cavern like a balcony. With his bionic eyes and his night-vision visor, Peri could see the floor of sheer ice at the bottom of the cavern. Extreme coldness radiated off it in waves that pulsed through him. It had to be the heart of the planet, and it was made of pure ice!

'I can see Peri,' Selene crackled over the radio. 'Quick!'

Peri spun around. He waved his arms and shouted to his friends, 'Slow down! The path ends in a precipice.'

Selene and Diesel skidded to a halt. 'Talk

about looking for a star and finding a black hole,' Selene said, peering over the edge at the massive drop to the frozen heart.

'I know,' Peri replied. 'I never would have believed anything like this could exist in the universe unless I saw it with my own eyes. It's cosmic-mind-blowing!'

Even Diesel took a sharp breath before saying, 'It's not bad. But I've seen more amazing things on Mars.'

Peri looked around. The bats had settled on the ceiling. They clung to the cracks in the ice. In the middle of the bats hung what looked like a giant stalactite of black ice. But as it came into focus, Peri realised it was a giant moon-bat. Its massive wings wrapped around its huge body. It looked as if it was sleeping, drool dripping off fangs the size of his arm.

'The moon-bat queen!' Selene gasped.

'*Ch'açh*,' Diesel muttered. The narrow band of hair under his helmet turned bone-white. 'I've never s-s-seen anything so scary in my life.'

'Let's g-g-get out of here!' Otto said. 'Before she w-w-wakes up and e-e-eats us!'

'No,' replied Peri, 'The bats brought us here for a reason.'

'Perhaps they wanted to freeze us,' Selene said as she shivered. 'This has to be the coldest spot in the whole planet.'

'That's it,' Peri exclaimed. 'It's the coldest spot and it's still melting. Remember they said "Flood"? All that drilling on the surface and the huge holes must have let heat and light reach the inside of the planet. It's getting too hot underground. The ice-heart is melting.'

'The moon-bats' natural habitat is

defrosting,' Selene said.

'If we want to save the moon-bats,' Peri replied, 'we have to somehow make this planet even colder!'

Chapter 7

'You're c-c-crazy!' said Otto. He could barely move. His arms, legs and neck had shrunk to almost human size from the cold. 'The b-b-bats are s-s-sleeping! We sh-sh-should run while we h-h-have the ch-ch-chance! Get off this fr-fr-freezing rock!'

Peri resisted the urge to push the bounty hunter over the edge of the abyss and leave him there. 'Our ship is repairing itself, so we can't leave,' he retorted. 'Besides, you need me to fly the ship. I say, we're not going anywhere until we save the moon-bats.'

'I've got an idea,' Selene said. She grabbed Diesel and spun him around.

'Hey, dumboid, what are you doing?' the gunner objected.

'Shh,' Selene replied, unzipping his podpack. 'Don't move. If I know the *Phoenix*, there should be something in here that will help.'

She started pulling stuff from the sleek pod on Diesel's back. 'Heal-u-like gel, nano-bandages,' she mumbled, delving deeper. 'Instant-fire grenades, no good. Martian-mosquito electro-nets, self-inflating sleep unit – no, no, no. Toe-amputator, definitely not. Ah! *This* will do!'

Selene pulled out a Swizaser. It didn't look like much. The compact laser was barely bigger than a hand and was made of a large sphere with two spikes. Selene gripped one of the spikes and aimed the other at the floor before flicking a switch. A narrow beam of burning hot light shot out. It zapped the ground. Steam rose as it vaporised damp stone. She switched it off and grinned. 'This could work.'

Peri shook his head. 'We need to *cool* the planet, not vaporise it!'

'It l-l-looks perfect for r-r-roasted bat!' Otto said.

'Will you shut up about eating moon-bats!' Diesel shouted.

Selene ignored them both, speaking directly to Peri. 'Obviously, we need a few adjustments.' She took off her gloves and clamped them between her knees, before fiddling with the sleeve of her Expedition Wear.

'Put your gloves back on,' Peri demanded, 'or you'll freeze to death.'

Selene shot him a withering look, although her hands were already shaking. She pulled a small tool from the watch band under her survival suit. Hooking the tool into a hidden nano-fastening, she popped the cover-panel off the Swizaser and dropped it at her feet.

Underneath the cover, the Swizaser was a tangle of wires and circuit boards, coloured tubes and buttons. Selene clipped wires from the device and dumped them on the upturned cover. It was like surgery. It sent a shiver through Peri just watching. He could imagine her doing similar things to his own bionic wires and circuits. He hoped she would never have to.

'Hurry up,' he said. There was a frown of concentration on Selene's face. She pulled

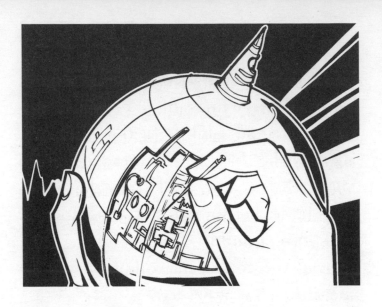

out a small circuit board, adjusted it with her tool and dropped it back inside. She was fast, despite her fingertips turning blue. 'You're going to lose your fingers if you don't warm up soon,' he warned her.

'Nearly there,' Selene replied as she started twisting the wires together. 'Got it!' She snatched up the cover-panel from the ice, tipped the spare wires into her pocket and closed up the Swizaser. She flicked the switches again. A beam of pure crystal blue light streamed out, smoking as it hit the damp ground. It was no longer a hot, vaporising laser beam. It was as cold as a comet.

'*Klûu'ah*,' Diesel exclaimed, snatching the Swizaser. 'You're not the complete cosmic wastoid you look.'

Peri dropped his podpack and pulled out his Swizaser. 'Here, Selene,' he said, handing it over. 'Do mine next. Otto, get your Swizaser out and hand it over,'

Selene swiftly finished Peri's Swizaser upgrade. Peri held Otto's Swizaser while she made the adjustments. Now that she knew what she was doing, Selene worked faster, but by the time she finished working on Otto's, her hands were shaking badly.

'Don't you think you should let yourself warm up first?' Peri asked. 'Before you modify your own Swizaser?'

'N-n-no t-t-time.' Selene's teeth were chattering.

She adjusted her own Swizaser last, working at double speed, before she grabbed the gloves from between her knees and yanked them on. She grimaced as she waited for her Expedition Wear to heat her up.

Peri aimed his Swizaser into the bottom of the cave and fired. The beam of freezing light lit up the cave, but it didn't seem to do anything. He was too far away.

'Everyone, copy me,' Peri said. 'If we —'

'Actually, Peri,' Selene interrupted, pointing to the cracks in the cavern's icy walls. 'I think we'd be better off freezing the walls first before they collapse.'

A piercing scream filled the air. The queen moon-bat had woken up and her eyes were blazing with fury. She opened her mouth and screamed again, the sound exploding through Peri's head. Instinctively, he slapped his hands to his ears, but could not reach them through the Expedition Wear helmet.

'Watch out!' Peri ducked as a bat tried to swipe at his head. The entire swarm of moon-bats had been woken by the queen. A tornado of wings, fangs and spikes swept down towards the crew.

'Why are they attacking? We're trying to help them!' Diesel yelled.

'How would they know?' Peri said. 'We just need to show we mean no harm.'

'Sorry, Peri, it's either them or us. We're going to have to freeze them,' Diesel yelled as he fired his modified Swizaser at the moon-bats.

Peri feared it would make them even angrier, but he was wrong. It was calming them down. Selene hesitated, but joined in

too. It was working! The cooling effect of lasers seemed to make the bats feel better.

'Keep firing at the moon-bats. It's help-ing!' Peri shouted as he realised what he needed to do. He tucked the Swizaser into his belt and pressed himself against the wall.

'What are you doing?' Diesel asked.

Peri didn't answer. He ran across the path and threw himself over the edge.

'I've got an idea!' he yelled as he plunged into the abyss.

Chapter 8

Peri fell towards the frozen heart of the cavern, tumbling against the walls of rock and ice as he fell. There was no time for his Expedition Wear to inflate.

Slllaaaammm!

He smacked into a giant slab of ice and crashed on to the slanted cavern floor. He slid towards a dark pool of freezing water. He clawed against the smooth ice, but it was slick with melted water. If he slipped into the icy pool, he didn't stand a chance of surviving.

'Come on,' he urged his suit. 'Help me.'

Instantly, his hands tingled and the gloves of his Expedition Wear began to buzz. Sharp ice-spikes sprang from the palms like shiny metal teeth. More spikes appeared on his knees and the toes of his boots.

'Rocket-tastic!' Peri exclaimed.

He slammed his spiked gloves and boots into the ice. Cold splinters flew everywhere and he stopped sliding. Peri stared at the huge peaks of ice jutting up from the glowing blue-green ice at the heart of the planet. He needed to fire directly into the ice-heart if there was even a chance his modified Swizaser could heal it. He needed a direct line of sight.

Peri clawed upwards, away from the pool of freezing water. The ice creaked and moaned under his weight. Small fissures grazed the surface as he kept spiking into the ice. He was almost at the top of the block. Another arm's length and he'd be in the perfect spot.

Eeeraaa-craaack! The block of ice snapped and started tipping backwards. He used his spiked toes to launch himself over the ice.

Craaasssh! The block smashed under him as he landed, spraying water and ice over him like an exploding galactic snow cone. A wave of freezing slush slapped his suit.

'Peri?' Selene called over the radio. 'Are you OK?'

Peri glanced up. An icy fog from cold Swizaser-blasting filled the top of the cave. He couldn't see his friends – or Otto.

'I'm OK,' he radioed back. 'Keep firing!'

He wasn't going to get a clearer shot at the glowing heart than this. He was standing on it. He pulled the Swizaser from his belt and fired the brilliant blue beam at the

slush under his feet. Instantly, it turned
into ice. Glimmering crystals spread out
from where he had aimed. He stepped back
as the ice tried to freeze around him.

The icy heart of the moon-planet was
expanding beneath his boots. Cloudy
vapour swirled around Peri as the ice
pushed him up. He was doing it. He was
saving the planet! He glanced at the ceiling

to see how much more ice was needed to fill the heart. But instead of seeing the moon-bats or their queen, he saw ice crowding in over him.

What's happening? he wondered, as a shiver of panic ran through his body. His crew had been firing at the bats to keep them calm, but it must have chilled the air at the top of the cave. Ice had formed on the path around the cavern. It was stretching out to create a dome over the icy-heart. If he wasn't careful, he was going to be entombed in the ice!

'Selene,' Peri said over the radio. 'Stop firing!'

'What?' Selene asked. 'Why?'

'Because you're going to trap me if you don't,' Peri said.

He blasted the ground beneath him again. The icy-heart growled and moaned but it was healing and growing larger. He could feel it lifting him towards the middle of the cave.

Creeaaack! The noise ricocheted around him. Peri looked up. The partially formed dome of ice was breaking. A huge block sheared off right above him. He leapt aside as it shattered against the heart.

Peri gasped as splinters of ice pelted his helmet. If he'd been underneath the block, it would have split him in two.

Creeaaack!

More lumps of ice were breaking away from the walls. As they crashed down, Peri slid and dived out of their way, narrowly avoiding being pounded into space-mash. He dodged the deadly ice missiles and continued to blast the floor. No matter the danger, he couldn't leave unless the planet's heart was healed.

But it was difficult to dodge and fire at the same time. The ground was still rising. It absorbed the shattered ice into its cloudy white bulk. He was almost there. The heart appeared to be expanding on its own. It must be cold enough to generate its own ice. It kept pushing him up higher and higher. It was now level with the path around the cave, but it was still going.

Peri half ran and half slid across the surface towards Diesel and Otto. The ice was beginning to rise around them.

'Nice going!' Selene gave him a high five. 'I think we should help the icy-heart reach the ceiling so it can stay cold and not melt again.'

'Everyone, fire!' Peri commanded.

Selene and Diesel raised their Swizasers. Even Otto helped. Four beams of fierce cold chilled the heart, making it glow brighter and brighter. Cold radiated off it in pulses like heat from the sun. The mass of ice pressed forward, threatening to crush Peri and his crew into the wall.

'Quick, back into the tunnel!' Peri yelled.

As the crew raced into the tunnel, ice blocked the entrance to the cavern behind them.

'We've done it!' Peri cheered.

Peri and his crew switched off their Swizasers. The heart lost its cloudy appearance and took on a pure crystal-blue shine. Inside the ice, they could see moon-bats making new tunnels with their spiked wings.

'Wow,' Peri exclaimed, 'look at them go. The moon-bats must live and hibernate inside the ice. Their wings are for flying but they can also tunnel through ice.' Despite the cold pouring off the ice, a beam of warmth hit their bodies.

'*Ch'aḉ*,' Diesel exclaimed. 'Do you feel that?'

'Shh, listen,' Peri ordered. It was hard to hear, but somehow through all the ice and rock, there was a message being sent to them. As he focused on the warmth soothing his body, Peri finally understood what it was. It was a message from the bats and their queen – two words repeated over and over: 'Thank you. Thank you. Thank you.'

Peri slumped to the floor alongside the others.

'Rest for a bit,' Selene said. 'But then we've got to find our way out.'

'Hopefully the *Phoenix* will be repaired,' replied Peri. 'Maybe it can help seal the holes in the planet's surface to stop the ice melting again, but I don't know how we even go about finding –'

Before Peri could finish his sentence, a

rumbling filled the tunnel. The ice was still expanding and grinding its way down the tunnel towards them. As they scrambled to their feet and backed away from the danger, Peri noticed the water on the floor was freezing.

'We're going to be cr-cr-crushed to death!' Otto screamed. He fired his Swizaser, before remembering it had been modified to make things colder. 'Stupid thing!' he cried, throwing it at the wall.

'I don't understand,' Diesel muttered. 'I thought we saved the planet.'

'Why didn't I think of it before?' Selene said. 'It's not a single column of ice, but the whole core of the planet! The tunnels are like veins. They connect the ice to the rest of the moon-planet. The ice is like blood. Now that the heart is back to normal . . .'

Peri finished her sentence. 'The ice will flow through all of these tunnels. We'll be frozen inside this planet unless we get out now!'

Chapter 9

The crew half ran, half slid through the tunnels. Peri's heart thumped as though trying to break from his chest and get away faster than he could. Every muscle in his legs ached from keeping him upright as he sprinted over the slippery ground. His space boots pounded against the floor, cracking ice as they did so. A wave of jagged ice crystals surged behind them. A nightmare of snow and ice and rock threatened to crush him and freeze him into a space-lolly. It growled and moaned like a snow monster from Pluto, ripping at the walls and ceiling.

Selene was a few strides ahead, leaving Peri and Diesel to drag Otto. The Meigwor's limbs had shrunk in the cold, stiffening and becoming slow to react. If the bounty hunter hadn't been pulled along, he would have been a goner.

'Come on, Otto,' Peri screamed. 'We're nearly there . . .'

Peri pushed forward, jerking the bounty hunter to move faster. The cascading ice was catching up with them. Sharp white claws sliced at their legs as they sprinted, threatening to grab and crush them. Peri wasn't sure they'd make it. The sound of cracking, roaring and grinding ice vibrated through the tunnels as the whole planet started to refreeze. Even the tunnel ahead was narrowing as ice formed on the walls and ceiling.

'Let's leave him,' Diesel shouted, blue sweat flicking against the inside of his helmet.

'We don't leave anyone behind,' Peri replied. 'Keep hauling.'

It was no good. The ice ripped Otto from their hands, then swept Diesel into its churning mass. Peri heard Diesel scream '*Ahra'ck'pha!*' before the ice smashed against his body. It knocked Peri flying. Coldness surged around him. A storm of ice rolled him over headfirst and blocks of ice smashed his body one way, then another.

'Watch out, Selene,' Peri shouted.

But all he heard in response was a yelp of surprise. The mammoth tidal wave of ice must have swept Selene off her feet too.

Peri's Expedition Wear hissed and whirred, fighting against the ice to inflate. It softened the unseen blows as he was

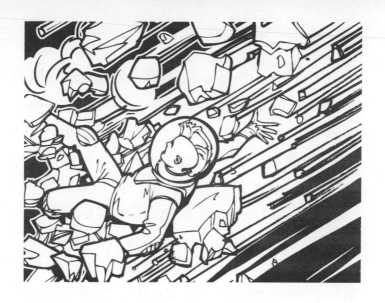

bashed and tossed about. The ice spun Peri over. His helmet smacked against the tunnel ceiling. He panicked, thinking that it had damaged his circuits. But a dim light flashed a warning inside the helmet. His night-vision visor had taken a hit.

'I can't see!' he shouted.

'My helmet's malfunctioning too,' Selene said.

'And mine,' Diesel grumbled.

The ice pushed Peri on in total darkness.

He could feel himself accelerating through the tunnels at incredible speed. It was like being in some alien rocket launcher, propelled along through a firing-tube before exploding into space. He felt as though he was moving faster than the *Phoenix* ever flew. Beyond Superluminal. If it wasn't for the inhuman sound of the ice as it gnawed into the stone and destroyed everything in its path, it might have been fun.

But it wasn't. Because Peri didn't know how long he would survive. The fast-flowing ice was crushing him against the hard black rock above, pushing his Expedition Wear to the limit. How much longer could it protect him? The only thing left to do was hope for a miracle.

Suddenly, the pressure against the suit vanished. He still couldn't see, but he could feel that the ice was lifting him upwards now instead. He had to be in one of the shafts which led to the surface.

'We're rising!' Selene shouted. 'I think I can see something.'

Peri peered upwards. His night-vision visor still wasn't working, but Selene was right. He could see the edges of a hole at the top of the shaft. He shook his head, not quite believing what he saw. Perhaps it was just wishful thinking.

Then he saw Diesel roll past. He wasn't in full colour, but it was definitely his grey silhouette. Natural daylight was filtering through the network of tunnels above them. They were being lifted to the surface of the moon-planet.

The ice pushed up and up, and the light grew stronger. Peri recognised the shaft they'd fallen through into the labyrinth of tunnels. 'We're going to be OK,' he said.

The planet seemed to know it, too. A surge of energy burst behind him, hurtling him up towards daylight. Like a sonic boom, Peri was thrown high, away from the hole into the air. Chunks of ice were flung around him like a blizzard.

Peri hit the sandy ground with a huge *thud!* It took him a moment to get his breath back and look around for his companions. Diesel had landed headfirst in a bank of the soft, powdery sand. Selene was trying to pull him out.

'We made it!' Peri whooped, jumping into the air.

He ran over to Selene and grabbed hold of Diesel's belt. As they pulled, Diesel kicked against them, trying to wriggle free.

'Hold still,' Peri yelled. 'We're trying to help you.'

'Help?' Diesel shouted. 'You're going to pull my head off.'

Selene grinned at Peri. They gave one more mighty tug. Diesel popped from the sand like a meteor blasted from a galactic pressure pipe.

'*S'fâh,*' Diesel snorted as he tumbled over. 'And I thought the ice was bad enough.'

'I was scared too,' Selene said. 'I really thought we weren't going to make it.'

'I didn't say I was scared,' Diesel snapped. 'I mean, that was the coolest ride in the universe! We should try to do it again.'

Peri rolled his eyes. Diesel never changed, but he was very glad they had made it out alive. He could see the *Phoenix* up ahead. There wasn't a single dent in the egg-shaped shell. The sleek white surface glistened in the sunlight as if the ship had never flown a single cosmic-centimetre. He didn't need a bionic link to the ship to know their vessel was fully repaired and ready to get back to their mission.

'Come on,' Selene said, shaking sand out of her podpack. 'We should get aboard and see how Prince Onix is doing.'

Peri couldn't wait to get back on the *Phoenix*, but he could feel something nagging in his belly like a Venusian stomach-eating-scorpion. 'Something's not right.'

'What do you mean?' Diesel asked. 'Did you forget to say goodbye to your batty friends?'

Peri stared blankly at his crew as he tried to make sense of the feeling. He had forgotten something.

Then he realised *who* was missing. 'Where's Otto?'

Chapter 10

'Down here, E-e-earthling!' Otto stuttered. He was trapped from the waist down in ice. His frosted arms strained as he tried to lift himself out, but they were weak with cold. The Meigwor was shivering uncontrollably. 'G-g-get me o-o-out of here, n-n-now!'

Peri tried not to giggle, but Diesel was howling with laughter. Blue tears ran down his cheeks.

'Well, this is lucky,' Selene said with a smile on her face. 'We can just leave him here – thanks to this rocket-tastic planet.'

'You can't leave me here!' Otto shouted. 'Typical of an inferior species to –'

Diesel shook his head. 'You deserve it. It's probably *Ving Tenal*.'

Peri had never heard that expression before. 'What?' he asked.

Diesel sighed. 'Don't they teach newbies anything? Planets aren't just lumps of earth and water orbiting suns. They have *Ving Tenal*. It's hard to understand, if you're not an expert in Martian, like me. This planet looked after the three people who tried to protect it, but not the one person who didn't want to help. The planet must have heard everything he said about eating the moon-bats and decided to get its revenge. The planet has *Ving Tenal*.'

'Nonsense!' Otto shouted, wriggling furiously. 'Planets are not alive. Stupid, superstitious, nonsense! Now stop talking and g-g-get me out of here, space-monkeys!'

Peri and Selene each grabbed one of Otto's long arms. 'Careful!' Otto growled.

'Stop being a space-baby,' Selene muttered. 'On the count of three. One, two, three!'

Peri tugged with all his strength. It was hard work. The Meigwor really was stuck. Peri's muscles strained as the ice gripped Otto, but he could feel him slowly coming free. With a cry of triumph and relief, Otto exploded from the ground.

Peri and Selene were thrown back as Otto was flung over their heads. The Meigwor-shaped ice hole sealed itself with a *craaccc-tuuutp!*

'Freezing, horrible planet!' Otto grumbled as he picked himself up and stormed towards the ship. 'Just you wait! When I'm w-w-warm again I'll show you space-monkeys a th-th-thing or t-t-two . . .'

But the *Phoenix* refused to let Otto back in the gleaming ship, until the crew had caught up.

Peri hesitated before pressing his hand against the sleek surface, remembering how it had electrocuted Diesel when he tried to get back in. But the *Phoenix* was ready to go now. A ghostly green light traced his palm and a rectangular door appeared. It swung open, sending a ramp gliding down into the sand. 'Welcome back,' the vessel said as they climbed into the ship.

'Thank you,' Peri replied.

The ramp retracted and the door closed. *Whiiirrr.* Air blasted from every direction, dislodging sand from the Expedition Wear. Peri led the group along the moving walkway to the Bridge.

It's good to be back on board, thought Peri. As the door to the Bridge opened, Peri wondered if the moon-bats would be OK now. 'Selene, can we do something to seal the holes on the planet's surface?' Peri asked.

'No problem.' Selene grabbed the control panel. Her fingers flew over the rows of buttons and dials. 'I'm scanning the surface . . .' A small monitor popped up with an image of the moon-planet. It pinpointed the holes in the surface. 'Now I'm analysing the geological composition of the planet . . .'

'What?' Diesel asked.

'She's studying the rocks,' Peri explained.

'So I can create a compound that will seal the holes and fit in with the planet's natural materials,' Selene continued. 'The *Phoenix* will eject something like a planet-sized plaster that will eventually merge with the surrounding material. And I've just about...' She flicked a few switches and the ship shuddered. 'That's it. All done.' She activated the 360-monitor. 'There. All better.'

The crew stood amazed at the *Phoenix*'s handiwork. A spongy blob splatted on the edge of each hole and then stretched to cover the space completely.

'Let's make sure the bats are OK,' Peri said, taking the control panel from Selene. Peri punched a few buttons and the small monitor changed, showing a series of red blobs moving in criss-crossing directions throughout the planet. 'You can see on this infrared image, the moon-bats are rebuilding a network of bat-sized tunnels in the ice.'

Selene gave Peri a high five. 'Orbitastic!'

'I think you both are a little batty,' Diesel
muttered.

The *Phoenix* announced, 'Xion specimen
Prince Onix has been rejuvenated. He is
currently being revived.'

'Let's get to the Med Centre,' Peri
exclaimed. 'We need to convince Onix that
Selene meant no harm.'

Peri sprinted to the nearest portal. He
thought of the Med Centre and when the
portal hissed open, there was Prince Onix
climbing out of a stasis-pod, looking

dazed. The others crowded in behind Peri.

'How are you feeling?' Peri asked.

The prince reacted with horror. 'Stay away from me!' he shouted, jumping behind the stasis-pod. 'Don't come any closer! Or, I'll . . . I'll . . .'

'Calm down, wastoid,' Diesel said. 'It's only us.'

'All of you, stay back,' the prince shouted, looking wildly around. 'What have you done to me?'

'What do you mean?' Selene asked. 'It's us, Onix.'

'Onix? Who's he?' the prince muttered. 'I don't know any of you. Where am I?'

Great, Peri thought, *he's got amnesia! He doesn't know who he is!*

'What did you put in that Sleepez, Selene?' whispered Peri, moving slowly towards the prince.

111

But Onix was like a frightened animal. He backed up against the wall, looking for a way to escape. 'Stay away!' he screamed, trying to pull something off a silver control panel. 'I'll hurt anyone who comes near me. I don't care who you are, or who I am, just stay where you –'

Before he could say another word, Selene shot the prince with a sonic dart. Onix slumped to the floor, unconscious.

'What the lunar moon-base did you do that for?' Peri cried.

'Is he in a coma again?' Diesel asked.

Selene shook her head. 'He's just stunned. Look, he's obviously got amnesia. He's going to be a pain to look after. If he's asleep, he can't try to escape or hurt us.'

'But we're in enough trouble as it is,' Peri said. 'The Xions will execute us on the spot if we bring him back like this

– they'll think we've tortured him. How can we return him when he doesn't know who he is?'

'Leave the stinking Xion on this rock and forget about him!' Otto boomed.

'No,' Peri said. 'We didn't leave you when we could, so we're not going to do it to Onix. And, Selene, I want you to promise not to shoot or sedate the prince again. You too, Otto.'

Peri stared at Otto and Selene until they reluctantly nodded. Two mechanical arms appeared and lifted the prince back into the stasis-pod.

'You're making more trouble for yourself, Earthling!' Otto muttered.

'I know,' Peri replied. 'It's not going to be easy, but doing the right thing isn't about doing the easiest thing. We just have to be ultra-careful from now on.'

As Peri stepped through the portal back to the Bridge, he vowed to himself: 'I'm going to get the prince back to Xion. Then I'm going to find a way home before we land ourselves in even deeper trouble!'

Will Peri and the crew make it safely
to planet Xion?

Can they survive an encounter with
the terrifying Xio-Bot?

Find out! In . . .

Turn over to read Chapter 1

Chapter 1

Purple. That was all Peri could see. He closed his eyes. He opened them again and turned 360 degrees. One moment they had been cruising in the *Phoenix*, watching the stars like tiny diamonds shining in space, and then this purple haze had descended.

Purple all around. It was bright and blinding. Peri screwed his eyelids tightly shut. He could hear Selene, Otto and Diesel stumbling around the Bridge.

'*S'fâh!*' Diesel shouted. 'What did you do, Otto?'

'I did nothing!' boomed Otto. 'Everything's just gone purple!'

Peri felt a change in the motion of the *Phoenix*. It speeded up, and shifted course.

'Something's taken control of us!' Selene shouted.

'How?' Peri asked. 'How could they get past our shields?'

Selene cleared her throat. 'That may be

my fault,' she said. 'I sent Boomerang messages on Ultrawave – to find out if anything's left of the Milky Way after the Xion attack. It's supposed to come back with replies attached. Something must be piggybacking on the return signal, using it to hack into our computer – and control us.'

'Who would do that?' Diesel asked.

'Take your pick,' Peri said. 'The Xion and the Meigwor have both sworn to destroy us.'

'I don't think any Meigwor is smart enough to pull this off,' Diesel replied.

Peri heard a *swish*, and *crack*, then a bellow of pain from Otto. He must have swung a punch at Diesel and hit the wall – in retaliation for the comment about his home planet.

'Missed!' Diesel jeered.

'We don't have time for fights,' Peri said. 'We need to take back control of the *Phoenix*.'